DREAMLAND

KID'S
5th Activity Book

Age 7+
Science

Compiled by :
Shweta Shilpa

Published by :

DREAMLAND PUBLICATIONS

J-128, KIRTI NAGAR, NEW DELHI-110 015 (INDIA)
PHONE : 011- 2510 6050, FAX : 011- 2543 8283
E-mail : dreamland@vsnl.com
Shop online at www.dreamlandpublications.com
Like us on www.facebook.com/DreamlandPublications

Published in 2014 by

DREAMLAND PUBLICATIONS

J-128, Kirti Nagar, New Delhi - 110 015 (India)
Tel : 011-2510 6050, Fax : 011-2543 8283
E-mail : dreamland@vsnl.com, www.dreamlandpublications.com

ISBN 978-81-8451-656-2
Printed by
Paras Offset Pvt. Ltd.

PREFACE

This 5th Activity Book is indeed a treasure house of fun filled moments. Every page of this book is full of entertaining assignments for children. This book on **"Science"** will enhance the child in grasping and understanding about the basic concepts of the Science.

Children will find the book interesting by involving themselves in solving mazes, adding colour to the drawings, matching the pairs, etc., and will have fun with dots and puzzles. At times, they may have to complete half-finished sketches or spot differences between pictures that almost look alike, thereby giving them a chance to think cohesively.

An attempt has been made not only to entertain but also stimulate the child's thinking, reasoning and creativity.

This book aims at providing children with a way to relax after a strenuous day of vigorous outdoor activity.

—**Publisher**

MEALTIME

Mr. Parrot loves to eat. There is so much food on the table. Help Mr. Parrot to categorize What is for **BREAKFAST** (B) and **DINNER** (D)

Butter ◯

Soup ◯

Cake ◯

Milk jug ◯

Green beans ◯

Toast ◯

Cereals ◯

Peas ◯

Fruit ◯

Tea ◯

Poached ◯

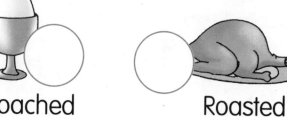
Roasted Chicken ◯

Bread-basket ◯

Name the Season You'll Be In
Pick up the clues and match it with the season they correctly belong to.

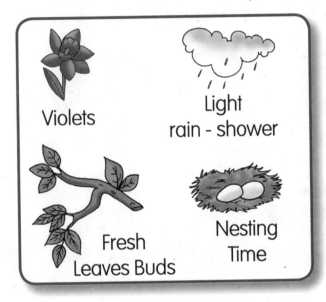

Violets

Light rain - shower

Fresh Leaves Buds

Nesting Time

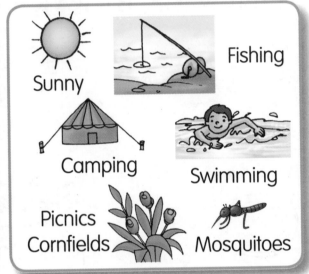

Sunny

Fishing

Camping

Swimming

Picnics Cornfields

Mosquitoes

AUTUMN   WINTER

SUMMER   SPRING

Skis

Snow

Snowman

Sleigh

Christmas Trees

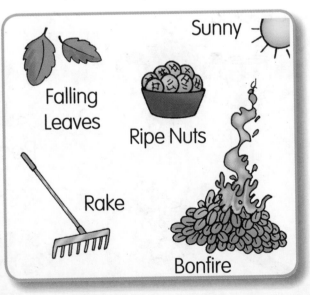

Sunny

Falling Leaves

Ripe Nuts

Rake

Bonfire

What Am I Made Up For?
Find the correct match from the clue box given below.

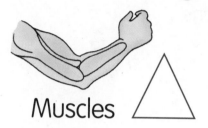

Muscles △

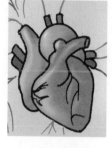

Heart △

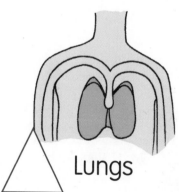

Lungs △

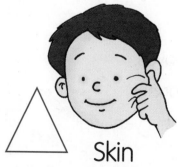

Skin △

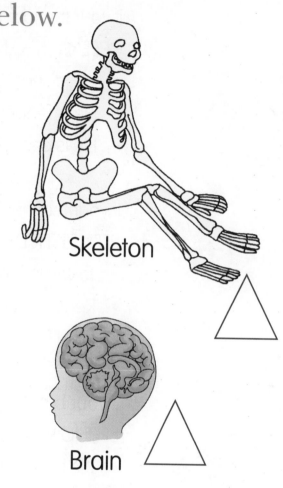

Skeleton △

Brain △

Clue Box

A. Is a framework
B. To pump blood
C. Covers and protects you
D. Moves the body
E. Is the control centre
F. To breathe oxygen

It Means.... Colour Speaking!

If your friend says he is
GREEN WITH ENVY it means...

- He is seasick.
- He is jealous.
- He is choking.

If your teacher says today is a
RED LETTER DAY it means...

- Today is Monday.
- Report- Card receiving day.
- Health check up day.

If your brother says he is
SEEING RED it means...

- He is angry.
- He is wearing glasses.
- He is suffering from eye infection.

If your mother has a
GREEN THUMB it means...

- She is wearing gloves.
- She has a lot of money.
- She can grow plants very well.

Jewels of the Solar System

	Has water and atmosphere and is perhaps the only planet with suitable life conditions.
	Is the biggest amongst all planets.
	Is closet to the sun.
	Is glowing and the hottest planet.
	Is the red planet.
	Is sadly not considered a planet anymore.
	Wears a ring of gases and is the second largest planet.
	Is named after the Roman God of the sea and begins with the alphabet 'U'.
	Was the first planet to be discovered with a telescope.

Invention Bubble

Connect the Invention Bubbles to their Inventor.

Thomas Alva Edison

Einstein

Galileo

Newton

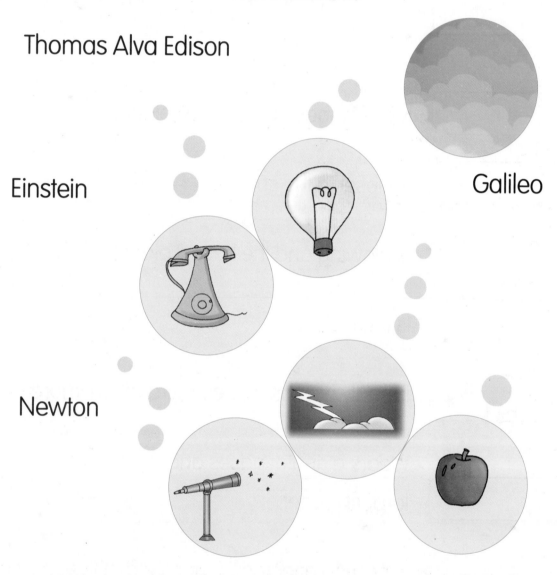

Alexandra Graham Bell

Wright Brothers

ADVENTURE GALORE

Scuba-diving, River-rafting, Ballooning, Moutaineering, Hang-Gliding, Bungee-Jumping.

Birds Brain

Large water bird with a pouch below Its beak to hold the Fish it catches.

A large ground bird with a long tail, is shot for sport fun and food.

Flamingo
Vulture
Pelican
Pheasant
Falcon

A pink long-legged bird with webbed feet.

A bird of prey that catches small birds in flight.

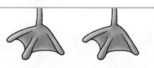

One of the largest birds. A scavenger.

Famous Said Proverbs
Check your knowledge with these proverbs. Match them with their latter half.

Jack of all trades	Troubled waters
Out of sight	The mice will play
To pour aid on	Out of a molehill
Charity begins	Master of none
To make a mountain	Out of mind
East or West	Saves nine
When the cat is away	At home
A stitch in time	Home is the best

Flag Quiz
Recognise the countries the flags belong to.

A U _ _ _ I A

_ A _ A _ A

_ _ I _ A

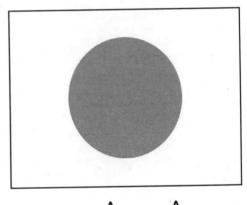

_ A _ A _

U _ I _ E _ _ I _ _ _ O _

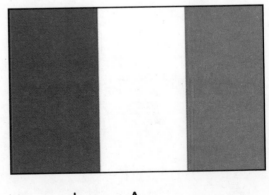

I _ A _ _

Making Secondary Colours

Name the two basic primary colours which when mixed together give us the new colour.

Make orange

Make grey

Make green

Make pink

Make violet

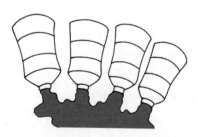

Make brown

In the City

Look around your surroundings. Can you place the clues with the places where they can be found.

Subway Platform
Underground entry
Metro – train

Bus
Police - car
Taxi van zebra - crossing
Traffic - lights sign – boards

Movie usherer
Pop - corn
Ticket window
Screen
Auditorium

Restaurant
Book – shop
Newspaper – stand
Telephone - box
Chemist

THEATRE

METRO-STATION

STREET

MAIN-ROAD

National Sports

COUNTRY	NATIONAL SPORT	PICTURE CLUES
Australia	....	
Canada	....	
Japan	....	
India	....	
Spain	....	
U. S. A	....	
Russia	....	
Scotland	....	

Help Box

Bull – fighting, Judo, Ice – Hockey, Cricket, Hockey, Chess, Baseball, Rugby, Football

Nature's Moods

TERMS	DEFINITIONS
Summit	dwelling of the Eskimos.
Dam	a piece of land surrounded by water on three sides.
Island	the highest point of a mountain
Igloo	violent shaking of the earth's surface.
Peninsula	a piece of land surrounded by water all sides.
Drought	an extremely large wave in the sea caused by an earthquake.
Earthquake	a barrier built across a river to control and block river water.
Cyclone	a place which has had little or no rain for a long period.
Tsunami	A violent tropical storm in which strong winds move in a circle.

Terminology

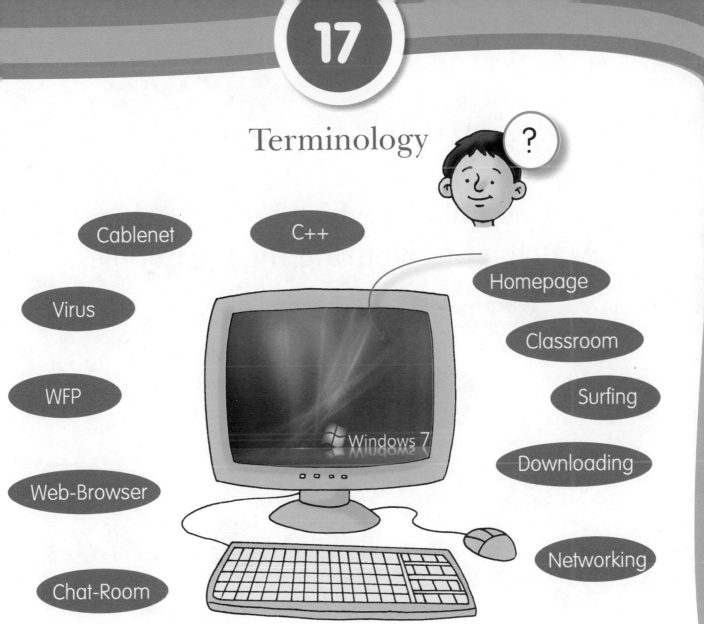

Cablenet

C++

Homepage

Virus

Classroom

WFP

Surfing

Web-Browser

Downloading

Networking

Chat-Room

The internet links thousands of computer networks around the world. Which of the above is the correct terminology used............feed into your P.C.. Some other terms......try matching them.

e-book   mailing through the computer.

e-text   electronic book.

e-mail   words and pictures.

PLACING IT RIGHT

Read the word- cluster and guess from the coloured bubbles which belongs where ?
Match it by colouring the big bubble.

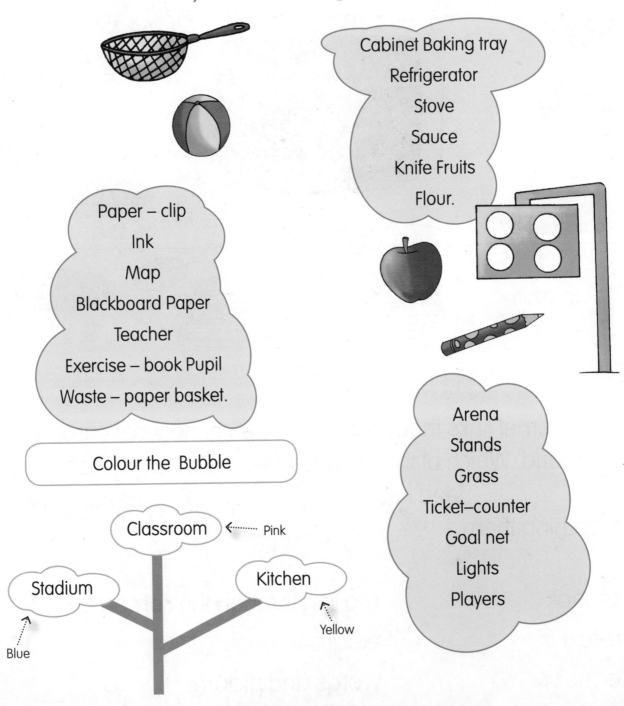

Cabinet Baking tray
Refrigerator
Stove
Sauce
Knife Fruits
Flour.

Paper – clip
Ink
Map
Blackboard Paper
Teacher
Exercise – book Pupil
Waste – paper basket.

Arena
Stands
Grass
Ticket–counter
Goal net
Lights
Players

Colour the Bubble

Classroom ←······· Pink

Stadium

Kitchen

↑
Blue

↑
Yellow

Heavy Metal

Ships are built here

Cars are repaired or assembled here.

Metals are melted here and separated from the raw ores.

Huge floating stations anchored on the sea – bed where oils are extracted from the oil bearing rocks in the sea.

Heavy machinery is built or repaired here.

Rigs

Dockyard

Garage

Factory / Workshop

Foundry

ANIMAL QUALITIES
Pick up two qualities of each animal.

An ANT ....

A SPIDER ....

A BUTTERFLY ....

A GRASSHOPPER ....

A LEOPARD ....

A VULTURE ....

A DOG ....

A LADYBIRD ....

HARDWORKING	GREEN	HAIRY
RED-LADY JUMPY	BLACK	COLOURFUL
DOMESTICATED	UGLY	PRETTY
CRAWLY	FEROCIOUS	CARNIVORE
SCAVENGER	MAN'S FRIEND	BUG

We are the LARGEST on the Earth

LARGEST DESERT

_____ (clue : In Africa)

LONGEST RIVER

_____ (clue : In Africa)

LARGEST LAKE

_____ (In Asia)

LARGEST OCEAN

_____

GREATEST WATERFALL

_____ (In Venezuela)

LARGEST ISLAND (IN AREA)

_____ (In N. America)

HIGHEST POINT ON EARTH

_____ (In Nepal)

WORD BANK

Nile
Mount Everest
Pacific Ocean
Sahara
Greenland
Caspian Sea
Angel Fall

Word it Right!

Shows the days, week, and months of a year.

(a) Calender .... (b) Calandar

Day after today

(a) Tomorrow .... (b) Tommorrow

Feeling full

(a) filing .... (b) filling

A vegetables with thick green leaves.

(a) cabbage .... (b) cabagge

A tool to cut vegetables and fruits.

(a) nife .... (b) knife

Polite and elegant

(a) gracius .... (b) gracious

BUILDINGS

F

S

W

S

C

COMMON ABBREVIATIONS

MM	=	Water
Kg	=	British Broadcasting Corporation.
BBC	=	Intelligence Quotient
UNO	=	Kilogram
USA	=	Oxygen
IQ	=	Millimeter
MP	=	United Nations Organization
O_2	=	Member of Parliament
H_2O	=	United States of America

FRESHH!

Which of these are fruits or vegetables will you put in the juicer for preparing some sweet 'n' healthy juice?

Getting My System in Order!

Around the systems revolve a word collections that forms a part of the systems drawn in the centre. Circle them according to the denoted observed circles.

Skull

Pelvic Girdle

Hand-Bone

Arteries

Mouth

Wind-pipe

Nose

Pancreas

Carbon di-oxide

Large Intestine

Liver

Knee Socket

Stomach

Heart

Shoulder Bone

Backbone

Lungs

Femur

Inhale

Blood

Oxygen

Veins

Anus

Ribs

Small Intestine

THE TRUTH ABOUT MY BODY

My body is made up of trillions of cells and 65% water

False   True

The Sun's harmful rays can burn our skin, protect it with a sun – screen lotion on a hot sunny day.

False   True

My toenails grow faster than my fingernails

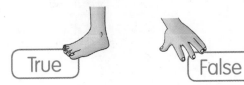

True   False

Exercise such as weight lifting makes our muscles bigger and stronger.

True   False

My brain always tells me what to do, even in danger my brain reacts faster than my body.

True   False

I can hear the sound of the sea in a seashell?

False   True

WORLD FACTS

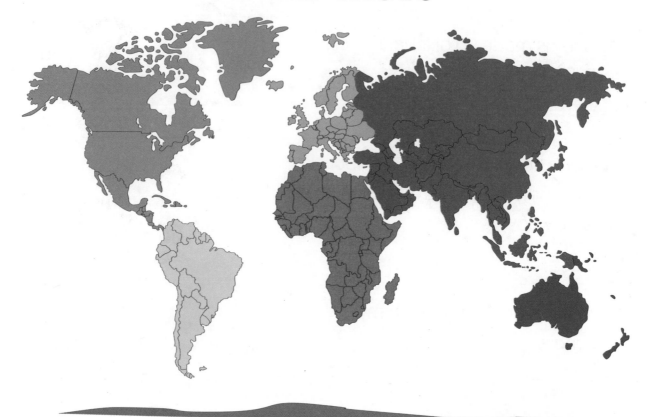

Place them in the above outline map of the world:

THE CONTINENTS

1. Asia
2. Africa
3. North America
4. South America
5. Antarctica
6. Europe
7. Australia

LARGE OCEAN

1. Pacific Ocean
2. Atlantic Ocean
3. Indian Ocean
4. Arctic Ocean
5. Southern Ocean

ALL WORK AND NO PLAY
Unscramble letters for the answers.

He flies an aeroplane OTIPL

He shows magic NIACIGMA

She looks after the patients in the hospital SERUN

He makes funny cartoon pictures / drawing to make any situation look funny OOTARCTSIN

He looks bakes 'n' buns, cookies 'n' cakes for you KEBAR

He makes and repairs shoes and slippers BLOCERB

He operates on people with a disease OENRUSG

Mowgli's Story

Here is Mowgli, the little kid from the jungle. He is telling you something about the wild life. Do you believe it or not ………. Colour the appropriate box.

Cheetah is the fastest land animal.

Believe it ☐   Do not believe it. ☐

A mosquito can carry blood almost double of its own weight.

Believe it ☐   Do not believe it ☐

Fireflies are light producing insects but also give electric shocks if touched.

Believe it ☐   Do not believe it ☐

Kangaroo balances itself with its feet and hands while running.

Believe it ☐   Do not believe it ☐

Starfish are called so because they fell from the sky.

Believe it ☐   Do not believe it ☐

For My Lit Dog… Pluto

Pluto forgot where he buried his tasty bone. Lets use the clues to help him… And scale to help us.

Start at the tree that exactly 1" tall.

Now move on to the nearest House.

Count the number of windows, from the front door go directly east that number of inches. Then turn and down south till you reach rock.

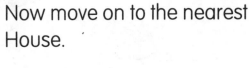

Go west from here. Do not get lost amongst the tree cluster.

Avoid it and turn down south.

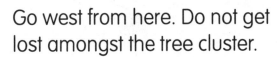

Follow the path of the house till the gate. Take a sharp U – turn and stop near the rock mount.

Great! You have found the place where the bone is buried.

WORLD FILE
Pick up on the clues to name the place (country/continent).

- CACTUS
- CORN
- SOMBRERO (HAT)

- GREAT BARRIER REEF
- THE ONLY – CONTINENT
- WHICH IS AN – ISLAND
- IS IN THE – SOUTHERN HEMISPHERE

- THIRD LARGEST COUNTRY
- GREAT WALL OF CHINA
- YUMMY NOODLES
- CHOPSTICKS

- PYRAMIDS
- STONE SCULPTURE
- THE SPHINX
- DESERT
- AFRICAN COUNTRY – OLDEST CIVILIZATION.

| EGYPT | MEXICO | CHINA | AUSTRALIA |

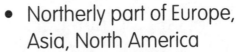

- The second largest continent
- Equator runs through its centre.
- Has the large Sahara Desert.
- Have a vast and rich reserve of animals and minerals.

- Northerly part of Europe, Asia, North America
- Freezing conditions.
- Home of Whales, polar-bears
- Home of Eskimos and other nomadic people.

- Made of 4 large islands
- Suffer very frequent earthquakes.
- Houses made from paper and bamboo to withstand earthquakes.
- Enjoy high standard of living, well developed technology.
- Bullet trains run on their railway network.

| AFRICA | JAPAN | THE ARCTIC |

Twenty Four Hours

Some clocks use a special way of telling time using 24 hours instead of the usual 12.

The day begins at 0000 and ends at 2359

e.g. number is 2359.

23 for hours 59 for minutes

Clues: When the hour has only 1 digit, a 0 is written before it. For all p.m. times, you add 12 to the number of hours.

NOW TRY IT OUT

4 : 02 A. M. ....

6 : 30 P. M. ....

2 : 00 A. M. ....

3 : 10 P. M. ....

9 : 00 A. M. ....

9 : 00 P. M. ....

10 : 10 A. M. ....

11 : 59 P. M. ....

PLAYGROUNDS

Where is TABLE TENNIS played?

....

Name the playground for WRESTLING.

....

What is playground for ICE- HOCKEY called?

....

What is a FOOTBALL playground called?

....

Where is BADMINTON played?

....

In the game of CRICKET what is the area between the

wickets called? ....

Where is game of BOXING played?

....

Arena

Field

Pitch

Table

Court

Ring

Rink

HOUSES

People live in different kinds of houses. If invited where would you find these houses?

Igloo ....

Tree house ....

Mud hut ....

Stone house ....

Houseboat ....

Block of flats ....

in the desert	in the forest	by the countryside
in the city	on ice	in the waterways

GALLERY

Follow the clues to name the famous personality and frame his name in the gallery.

Famous Egyptian queen, whose beauty was equally renowned

Queen of England under whose rule England became strong and prosperous.

He sailed across the Atlantic Ocean to find a sea route to the rich lands of the far east, however landed in the West – Indies.

The Russian cosmonaut, the first person to travel into space.

A. Yuri Gagarin B. Elizabeth I C. Cleopatra
D. Christopher Columbus.

Sybmology

Five colourful rings for an event that takes place every four years.

Symbol of Hospital or Medical Aid.

Two bones crossing each other diagonally with a skull signify.

Tying a black band around the forehead or the arm signify.

The colour of the flag flown on ships carrying patients with some infections disease.

A dove with an olive branch in its beak signify.

Danger / Yellow / Red Cross / Protest / Olympics / Peace

Special Terms

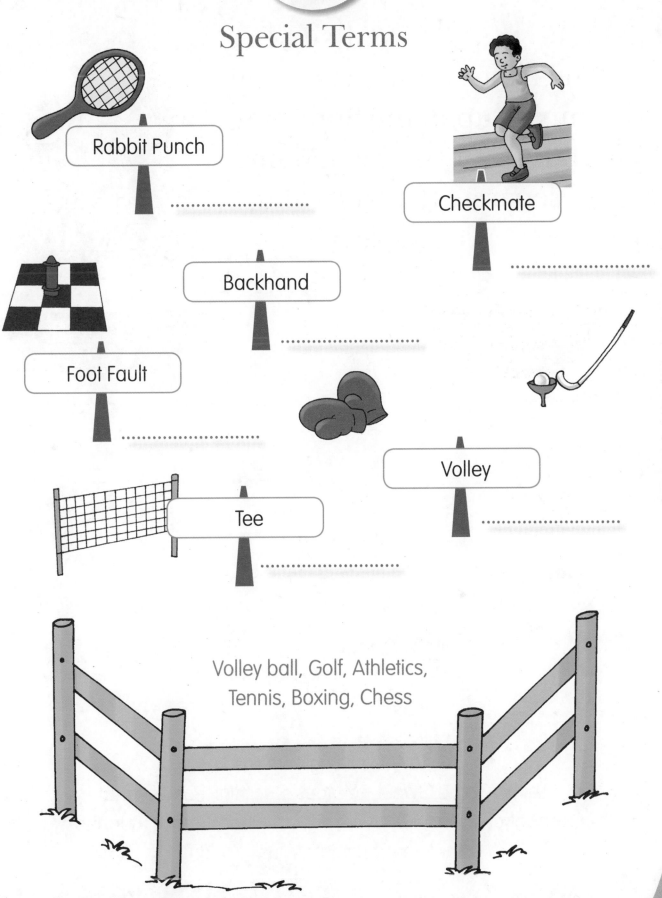

Rabbit Punch

Checkmate

Backhand

Foot Fault

Volley

Tee

Volley ball, Golf, Athletics, Tennis, Boxing, Chess

A Mixed Bag

The fruits and vegetables got mixed up in the Shopping Bag. Can you help Mama separate the fruits and vegetables.

....

....

....

....

....

....

....

....

....

....

Mixed Bag Contains
Lettuce, Lime, Sweet-Potatoes, Zucchini, Pomegranate, Grapefruit, Beets, Papaya, Spring-Onions, Berries, Bananas, Water-Chestnuts, Musk-Melon.

Be An Artist

Everyone likes to draw and paint. Collect the articles needed, pack up and let's go to the countryside for painting a landscape.

Canvas

Thread – Reel

Mixing Palette

Scissors

Paint Brushes

Story – Book

Paints

Binoculars

Easel

Where To Go?

To Egypt we shall go, to see the.

_____ _____

You shall fly to France to see the

_____ _____

A visit to London would enable us to see

_____ _____

Italy would finally give us a chance to see the

_____ _____

Eiffel - Tower   Great Pyramid   London - Tower.
Leaning Tower of Pisa

SPORT NUMEROLOGY
Specify the number of players in each side.

 FOOTBALL

 BASKETBALL

 HOCKEY

 TABLE TENNIS

 BADMINTON

 RUGBY FOOTBALL

11   5   11   2 or 4

            2 or 4   15

Beach-side Vocabulary

Surf-Board, Beach–Ball, Rowing–Boat, Towel, Picnic–Basket, Pail Learners Rubber- Tube, Swimming Costume, Sunglasses, Sun–tan Lotion, Sand–Castle, Sun-Umbrella, Oar Beach shorts, Spade.

The Sounds We Make!
Take your pick from these sound variety.

Army Bugle	Tick – Tock
Steam Engine	Tap
Raindrops	Creak
Clocks	Jingle
Boots	Ring
Coins	Whistle
Bells	Blow
Doors n' Hinges	Patter
Fire	Crackle

MY WORK TOOLS
Guess who uses what?

Stethoscope

 Egg Beater

Rolling Pin

Hammer

Cash Register

Meat Cleaver

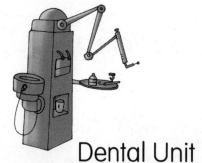
Dental Unit

Butcher

Carpenter

Dentist

Baker

Doctor

Cashier

Mother

COMPARISON AND CONNECTION
Yes ! Pair the opposites......

Long

Fat

Tall

Tiny

Small

Big

Short

Thin

THE STORY OF AIRCRAFTS
Try to put the development of these flying machines in order of evolution.

Montgolfier's
Balloon

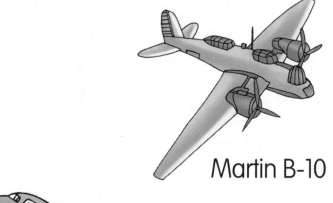

Martin B-10

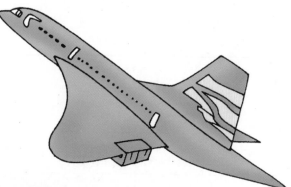

Boeing 747

Concorde

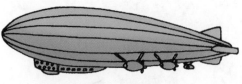

Graf Zeppelin II

The Smaller Portion with Greater Value…
Sentences and picture clues will help you fill in the blanks.

- I had a -------------------- of 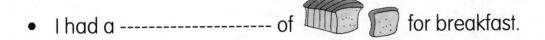 for breakfast.

- Please add a -----------------------of to the salad.

- Do not waste even a -----------------of  .

- Try not to overcook the --------------of the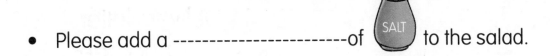

- The birds pecked at the small dry--------------------of the 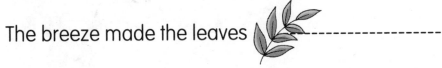 .

- The breeze made the leaves --------------------

- My ---------- in the biting cold of the snow.

- Thick ----- and lightning stuck during the storm.

PINCH   YOLK   SLICE   RUSTLE   THUNDERED
DROP   CRUMBS   CHATTERED

+ Science

50

PEOPLE WHO HELP US!

Grow food products

F _____

Delivers letters and packages

P_____

Cures us of teeth ailments

D _____

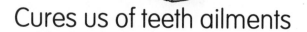

Constructs wooden items / furniture

C _____

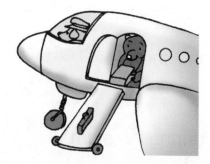

Can fly passenger planes

P _____

COLOUR BARS

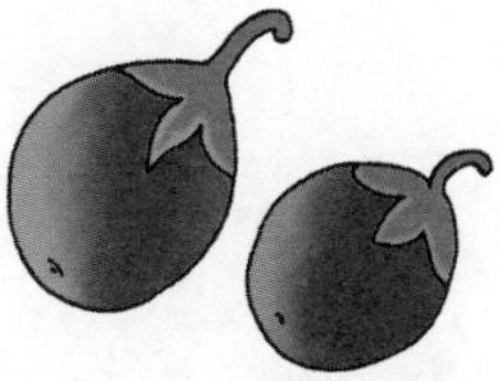

Eggplants are

Oranges are

Sunflowers are

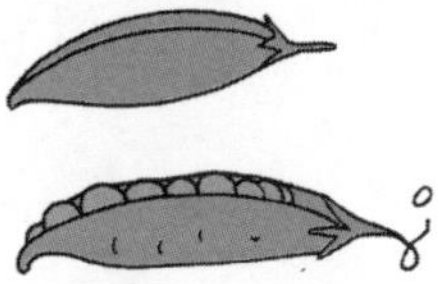

Peas are

Strawberries are

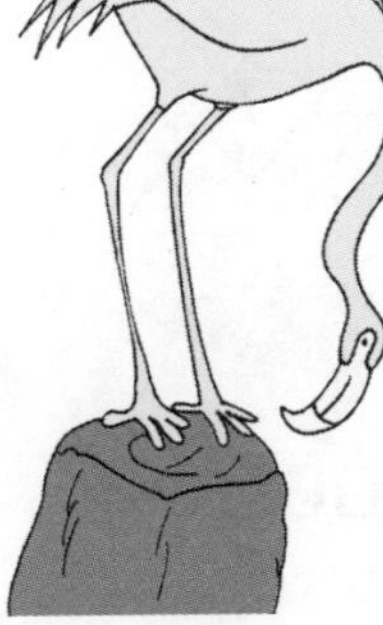

Flamingoes are

TOUCH
Match the textures.

Smooth

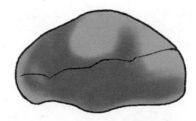

This is a piece of stone.

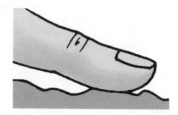

Rough

This is a piece of marble.

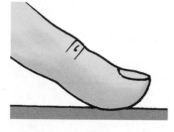

Soft

This is a hairbrush.

Hard

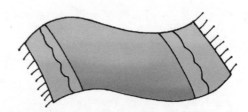

This is a silk carpet.

OUR PROFESSIONS
Would you like to be any of this when you grow up?

....

....

OFFICIAL RESIDENCES

The "first citizens" or the President / Prime Minister of a country live in the houses allotted by the country's government. Match a few mentioned here.......

President of America	Buckingham Palace
Queen of England	10 Downing Street
President of India	White House
The Pope	Rashtrapati Bhawan
Prime Minister of England	Vatican City

TRICKLE DOWN TO THE SOURCES

ITEMS	RAW MATERIAL	SOURCE

Shoes

Woollen Yarn

Cotton Plant

Breads

Leather

Grains

Woollens

Cloth

Sheep

Clothes

Flour

Skin of dead animals

Clay pots

Clay

River bed

Vowel Hunting

Recall the vowels in the series of English alphabets

—— —— —— —— —— Great!

Now go ahead and pick up the vowels in the words below... these could be more than just one also.

Olympic
—— ——

Opposite
—— —— —— ——

Hamburger
—— —— ——

Sesame
—— —— ——

Soldier
—— —— ——

Magnify
—— ——

Star
——

Dress
——

Ant
——

Umbrella
—— —— ——

Magic
—— ——

Pizza
—— ——

Nurse
—— ——

Glow
——

Surprise
—— —— ——

Special Places To Live

There are some special places used for or used by special people. Match the columns below to understand the above statement.

a. Monk   ◯ Hostel

b   Soldier   ◯ Camp

c. Student   ◯ Monastery

d. Scouts /Trekkers   ◯ Palace

e. Queen / King   ◯ Hospital

f. Nun   ◯ Barrack

G. Ill or injured people   ◯ Creche

h. Day Nursery   ◯ Convent
    for Toddlers / Young Children

Remember Your Nursery Rhymes?
Lets check…

Twinkle Twinkle Little_____

Mary Had a little_____

Incy Wincy _____

I'm a little_____

_____on the railway line.

Jack and Jill went up the_____

Rock a bye_____

1, 2, 3, 4, 5, Once I caught a _____alive.

PICTURE CLUES: CHANGE THEM INTO WORDS.

What Would You Not Like To See Here?

KITCHEN

Crockery Sink Tube light Filter Gas Cylinder Hanger Eraser
Untensils Video Cassettes Tap Lunch – Box Magazine – stand.

ON THE BIRTHDAY - PARTY

Soaps Paper dish Water-Bottle Rulers Cold-Drinks Caps Dish
–Washer Flowers Snakes Clown Candles Gifts Mixers Festoons.

IN THE PARK

Trees Bears Cassette Player See – saw Jungle Gym
Sandpit Ponds Ducks Rocking Chair Bench Fountain Slides
Swing Butterflies.

AT THE CIRCUS

Musician Bandage Unicyclist Magician Gifts Clowns Ants
Juggler Wheel-Chair Lion-Show Trapeze Horse Show Elephants.

What We Love To Dig In?

Yes! dig our teeth into our favourite foods.
Trace the path for these animals to pick up
and dig into their favourite foods.

Believe It or Not
Read these paragraphs. Tell which is correct and which not.

The Sun is a glowing ball of hot gases that contain the same chemical elements as found on the earth's crust.

Comets are villains of the solar – system. They have no orbit to travel on and on purpose go on destruction trail on other planets.

Stars that we see as pinpoints of light actually appear so because they are far away from us. The sun is the closest star to us. The rest of the stars are so large that could fill the space between the earth and the sun.

Amazing World
Number them according to size starting with the largest.

Penguins

Blue Whale

Honey-bee

Bats

Cat

Humans

Elephants

Musical Chatter
Riddles on musical instruments?

Just strum my strings or sing
along. Play rock 'n' roll or a
melodious song.

On hitting my top
You'll hear a clang
Now you've shook me
It's hard for me to stop.

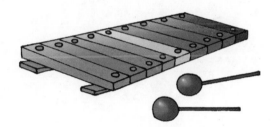

A long tube with holes
is what you'll think of me.
High sounds you'll hear
Just play on me.

Different sizes
Are my bars of wood
From high to low
Oooh! My tones sounds too good.

THE LAST WORDS OF THE DAY

All the animals here have the last word to say
before you close down this book. Guess who says what?

Mr. Pig	Mr. Dog	Miss Cat	Gruffly Bear

Miss Duck	Lil Mouse	Mr. Frog

Do you know what they are saying?

"Good - Bye!"

quack croak bow-wow squeek

oink meow gruff